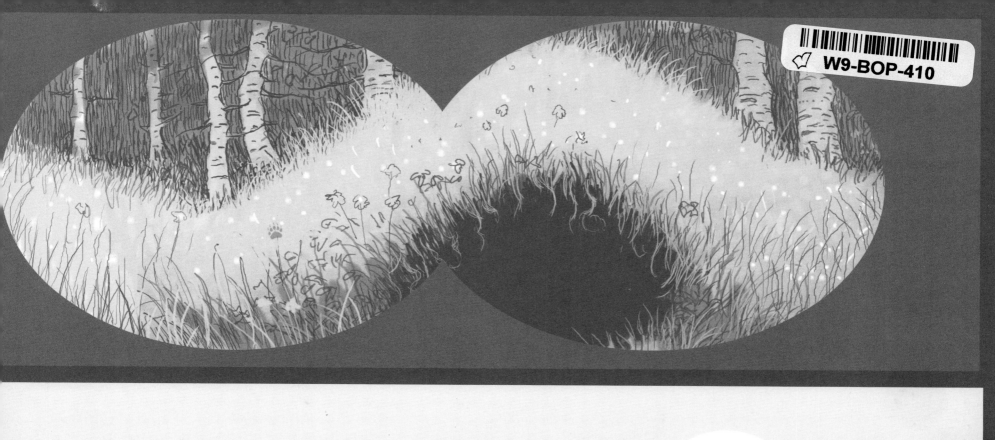

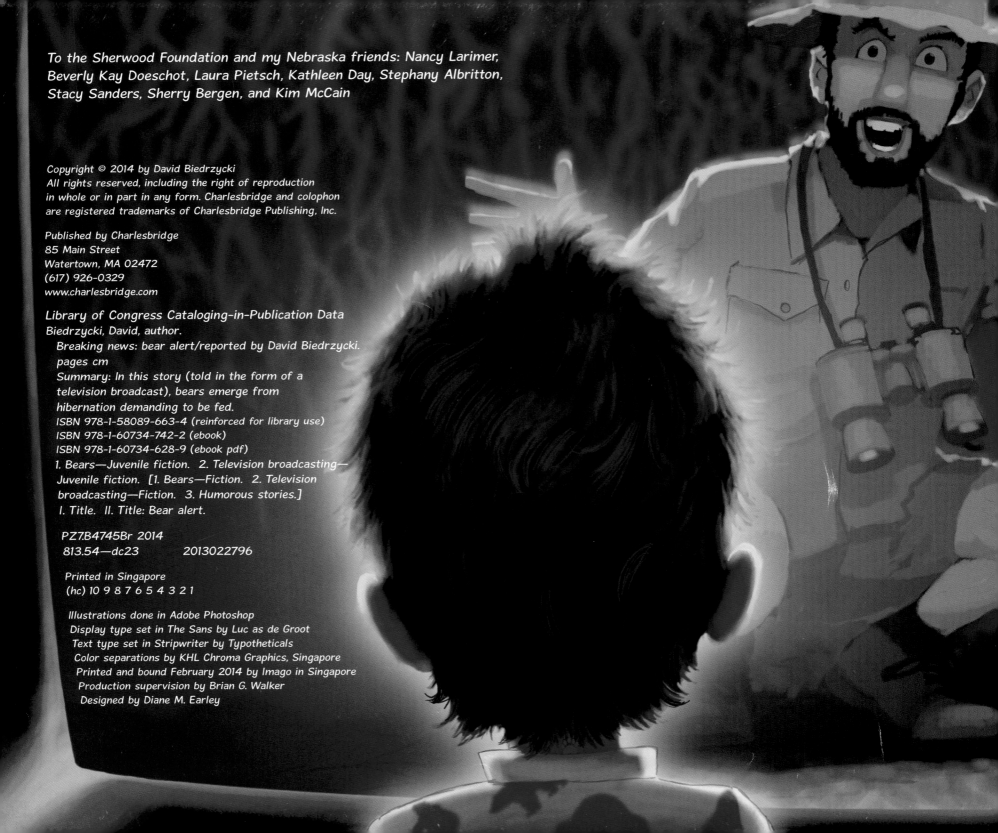

To the Sherwood Foundation and my Nebraska friends: Nancy Larimer,
Beverly Kay Doeschot, Laura Pietsch, Kathleen Day, Stephany Albritton,
Stacy Sanders, Sherry Bergen, and Kim McCain

Published by Charlesbridge
85 Main Street
Watertown, MA 02472
(617) 926-0329
www.charlesbridge.com

Library of Congress Cataloging-in-Publication Data
Biedrzycki, David, author.
  Breaking news: bear alert/reported by David Biedrzycki.
  pages cm
  Summary: In this story (told in the form of a
  television broadcast), bears emerge from
  hibernation demanding to be fed.
  ISBN 978-1-58089-663-4 (reinforced for library use)
  ISBN 978-1-60734-742-2 (ebook)
  ISBN 978-1-60734-628-9 (ebook pdf)
  1. Bears—Juvenile fiction. 2. Television broadcasting—
  Juvenile fiction. [1. Bears—Fiction. 2. Television
  broadcasting—Fiction. 3. Humorous stories.]
  I. Title. II. Title: Bear alert.

  PZ7.B4745Br 2014
  813.54—dc23   2013022796

  Printed in Singapore
  (hc) 10 9 8 7 6 5 4 3 2 1

  Illustrations done in Adobe Photoshop
  Display type set in The Sans by Luc as de Groot
  Text type set in Stripwriter by Typotheticals
  Color separations by KHL Chroma Graphics, Singapore
  Printed and bound February 2014 by Imago in Singapore
  Production supervision by Brian G. Walker
  Designed by Diane M. Earley

WE INTERRUPT THIS
STORY TO BRING YOU

BREAKING NEWS

BEAR ALERT

Reported by **David Biedrzycki**

BEAR ALERT **SKYCAM 3** NEWS HELICOPTER SHOWS TWO

BEARS ON TOP OF TRUCK HEADED DOWNTOWN.

TRAFFIC CAMERA CAPTURES SHOWDOWN. *BEAR ALERT*

ENTER

CAUTION

CAUTION CAUTION

WET CEMENT

Pooh St.

Main

DETOUR
BEAR RIGHT

ROUNDING THE CORNER OF POOH AND MAIN.

BEAR ALERT EXPERTS SAY BEARS ARE NATURALLY SHY AND

LOUD SOUNDS WILL SCARE THEM AWAY. *BEAR ALERT*

BEAR ALERT RESIDENTS ARE ASKED TO KEEP THEIR

BEAR ALERT ANIMAL CONTROL OFFICERS HAVE ARRIVED

Paddington's security video

Jewelry

DINGTON'S

BEAR ALERT BEARS LAST SEEN IN MISSES AND PETITES

SECTION OF PADDINGTON'S DEPARTMENT STORE.

BREAKING NEWS REPORTED BURGLARY AT PADDINGTON'S.

SKYCAM 3 SPOTS SUSPECTS FLEEING ON FOOT.

BREAKING NEWS BEARS NAB BURGLARS. SKYCAM 3

SHOWS POLICE CLOSING IN TO MAKE ARREST.

WE NOW RETURN YOU TO YOUR REGULARLY SCHEDULED STORY.

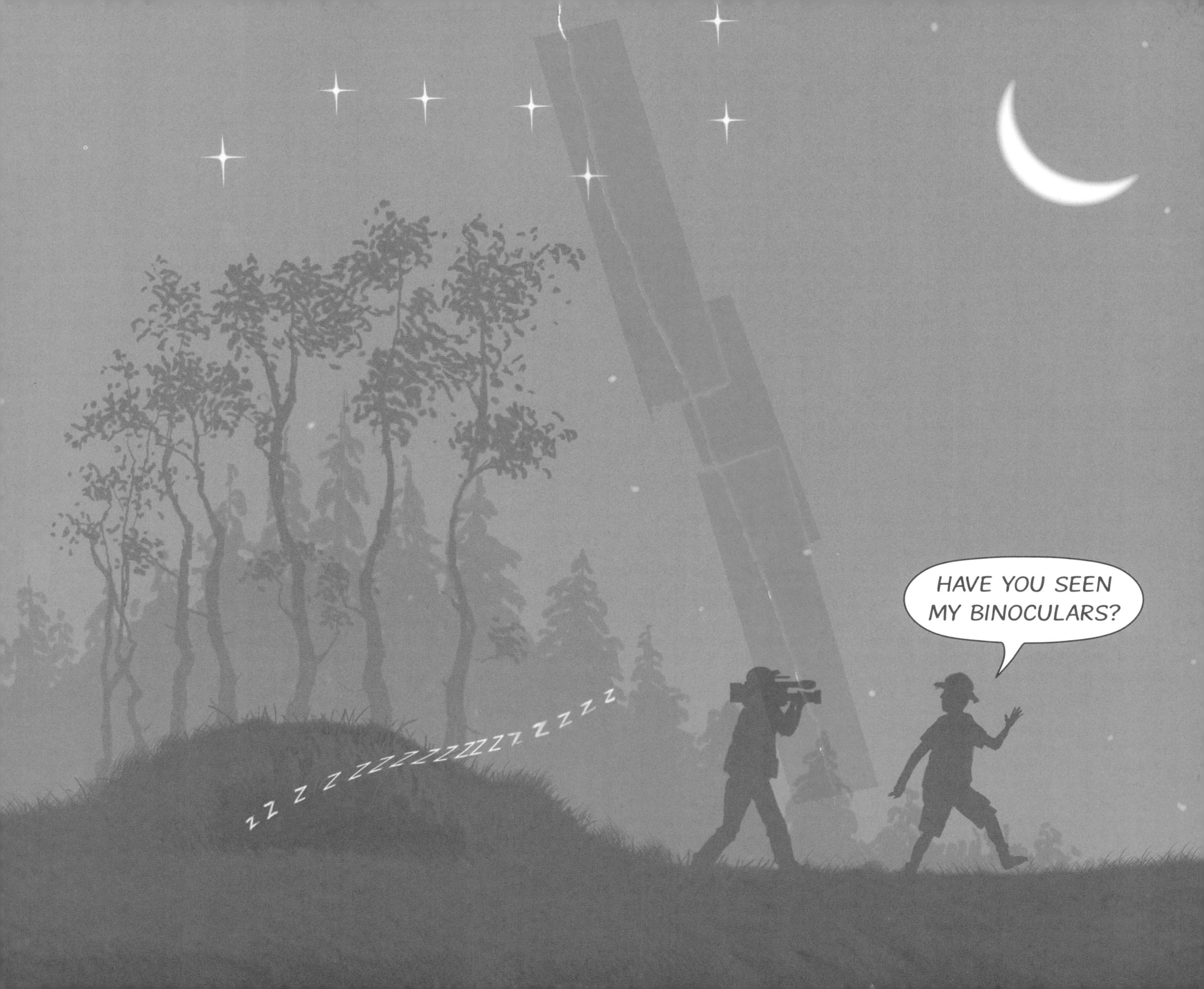
HAVE YOU SEEN MY BINOCULARS?